THE BRUSHMAKER'S DAUGHTER

A HOLOCAUST REMEMBRANCE
BOOK FOR YOUNG READERS

The Brushmaker's Daughter

KATHY KACER

Second Story Press

Library and Archives Canada Cataloguing in Publication

Title: The brushmaker's daughter / Kathy Kacer.
Names: Kacer, Kathy, 1954- author.
Series: Holocaust remembrance book for young readers.
Description: Series statement: A Holocaust remembrance book for
  young readers
Identifiers: Canadiana (print) 20200210092 | Canadiana (ebook)
  20200210106 | ISBN 9781772601381 (softcover) | ISBN
  9781772601398 (EPUB)
Subjects: LCSH: Weidt, Otto, 1883-1947—Juvenile fiction.
Classification: LCC PS8571.A33 B78 2020 | DDC jC813/.54—dc23

Edited by Sarah Swartz

Photos on page 114 and 118 used with permission from Yad Vashem.
Yad Vashem Photo Archive, Jerusalem, 671.

Printed and bound in Canada

*Second Story Press gratefully acknowledges the support of the Ontario Arts
Council and the Canada Council for the Arts for our publishing program.
We acknowledge the financial support of the Government of Canada through
the Canada Book Fund.*

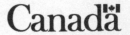

Published by
SECOND STORY PRESS
20 Maud Street, Suite 401
Toronto, ON M5V 2M5
www.secondstorypress.ca

*For Izzy, whose journey to read and learn
our history is just beginning.*

Chapter 1

It was just me and my Papa, running through the streets of Berlin in Germany, running for our lives. My small suitcase banged against my legs as I moved as quickly as I could, avoiding the streetlamps and the loud noise of traffic, trying to stay close to Papa and holding his arm. I breathed sharply, sucking in air and blowing it out in small puffs. My heart beat in my chest as fast as my breath came and went, maybe faster!

"Do you think it's this way, Papa?" I asked, trying to pull my father down a narrow laneway. I really had no idea where we were going.

"No, Lillian," he replied, resisting the tug and pausing a moment. His brow creased and he seemed to be listening for something; I didn't know what. "It's to the left," he finally said. And then, he began to walk in that direction, dragging me with him.

I hesitated. "Do you know where you're going?"

"I know."

I probably should have known better than to question him. I could see that his face was calm and determined. Papa was always steady. He knew exactly what to do and how to do it. And this was all the more astounding for the fact that he was blind and had been born that way. It amazed me how quickly and easily he could do just about anything—usually more easily than someone who had perfect sight! I adored him, my Papa. I loved how strong and proud and sure of himself he was. I loved that he always knew exactly how I was feeling without having to ask a single question, as if he could feel my feelings, as if he could *see* into my brain and into my heart.

"How do you do that?" I would ask whenever I watched him walk briskly on the street, prepare a meal, shop for groceries, get dressed in his suit with its matching tie that he could pick from his closet just by the feel of it, or a whole host of other skills. I had probably asked him that question a million times in my life.

Papa would smile. "Some people think being blind

is an obstacle," he would say. "I believe it's an opportunity to learn new things."

He had told me that a million times as well, but it still surprised me.

A siren sounded in the background. I startled, pressing closer to Papa as my heart rate picked up again. He placed one arm around my shoulder and drew me even nearer.

"We're fine," he said. "Keep moving."

This time, Papa's voice was not nearly as even. And as his face tightened, I couldn't shake the fear that pulsed through my body, rising from my feet into my stomach and up into my throat. There were Nazi soldiers everywhere on the streets of Berlin. And I knew they were hunting for Jewish people to arrest, like Papa and me. Things had been getting worse each day since that terrible man, Adolf Hitler, had come to power in Germany in 1933.

We had come from the city of Poznan in Poland, where I was born. There was a lot of prejudice against Jewish people everywhere, including in Poland. So, we left Poznan for Berlin. That was in 1937. Some would have thought we were heading toward a place that was even more dangerous for Jews than Poland. But Papa believed we could disappear into the big city where no one knew us. I was only seven years old at the time. I didn't ask questions. I trusted Papa as I always did. So, we left friends and family behind and came to Berlin.

"I believe it will be safer for us," Papa had said. And it had been for a while. We had managed at first to carry on with our new lives. We settled into a small neighborhood in Berlin called Kreuzberg, where there were only a few Jewish families, and we kept pretty much to ourselves. I went to school, and Papa worked in a textile shop.

But soon everything got worse. In November 1938, the windows of the synagogue where we sometimes went for Friday night services were smashed, and other synagogues across Germany were burned. We could no longer go to movie theaters, and valuables had to be handed over to the authorities. A year later, in September 1939, Nazi troops marched into Poland and declared war. A year after that, our radios and telephones were taken from us and we had to be off the street at sundown. Parks and playgrounds were off-limits to Jews.

And now it was 1941, and I was twelve years old. I was no longer allowed to go to school and no shops would serve Jewish customers. That's when the warning came that Jews could be arrested from their homes and deported by trains to prison camps in far-off places where people were starved, tortured, and even killed. That was worse than anything I had ever imagined. The world I knew was disappearing in front of my eyes, and there was nothing we could do about it.

After invading Poland, Germany had moved on to attack other countries across Europe, and the war was getting worse by the day. We had stopped hearing from friends and family members whom we had left behind in Poland. It was as if they had disappeared off the planet. And here we were, out on the streets of Berlin, running from our home and heading to a place that Papa said would be safe for us.

"Are you sure you know where we're going?" I asked again. I couldn't help myself. It was fear that made me question my father over and over.

"I know."

A motorcar suddenly came up behind us, revving its engine and screeching its tires. Papa grabbed me and pushed me behind a building, flattening us up against the wall and encircling me again with his arm. A cold sweat trickled down my back, and I shivered in the October evening air. Winter was coming. Soon, the snow would be on the ground here in Berlin. It was usually a time to play outdoors with my friends. If the snow was deep enough, we would make snowballs and throw them at each another, laughing and ducking when one came our way. But not now. There would be no laughter this winter. There would be no playing in the snow this year. And who knew for how long after that? I pulled my scarf tighter around my neck and tugged at the sleeves of my jacket, trying to cover my bare wrists. The jacket was too small for me, and had been too small for months. I hadn't had any new clothes in a long time, and I didn't know when I would.

The car passed, belching black smoke. "Wait one more minute," Papa said as I made a move to continue walking. A moment later, a second car passed.

"How did you know?" I whispered. My voice shook.

A faint smile passed over Papa's lips. "I hear and I know."

I paused, waiting for his signal. "Now, we can go," he finally said.

We continued moving, turning left down another laneway, then right across a quiet street, and then left and right again. The cobblestones pressed up into the soles of my shoes. Like my jacket, they were also becoming too tight on my feet. One lone streetlamp flickered on and off as we crossed another street and then veered down one last narrow lane and into a small courtyard. Buildings rose up on either side of us, swallowing the last bit of light from the street behind us. We ducked around two small trees. Up ahead and to one side was a gray door. Papa walked up to it as if he had always known it was there.

"We're here," he said.

Chapter 2

Papa knocked two quick raps. I shivered again, shifting my weight from one foot to the other as I looked around the darkened courtyard, unable to shake the feeling that someone was watching us. When would that feeling of fear end?

Meanwhile, Papa waited patiently, head tilted to one side, listening. Finally, we heard footsteps behind the door. A moment later it swung open. A man stood in front of us. His face was narrow, his dark hair brushed back off his forehead and slicked down with the same kind of hair cream that Papa often used—the kind that didn't allow a single hair to escape. He wore a gray suit and dark tie. A red handkerchief peeked out of his breast pocket. His eyes were curious and warm.

And even though I had no idea who he was, I felt my heartbeat slow down and my breathing return to normal, as if he had lifted some weight off my shoulders just by standing there.

"Otto Weidt?" Papa asked.

The man smiled a wide smile that stretched across his face. "Morris Frey!" he exclaimed. "Come in. I've been expecting you."

We entered into a tiny hallway and followed the man up a narrow set of stairs and into a small room. The wooden slats on the floor spread up the walls and to the ceiling where one lone lightbulb dangled and swayed back and forth, casting shadows across the man's face that appeared and disappeared with each swing. A sign high on the wall behind him read: Otto Weidt's Factory. I glanced at Papa as a dozen questions flew through my mind. But before I could ask a single one, the man began to talk.

"Did you have any trouble finding my place?"

Papa shook his head. "A few cars here and there that we avoided. But the instructions that you sent me after I had written to you were perfect."

Instructions? When had Papa received instructions? I knew that he often relied on a kind neighbor of ours to read and help respond to any mail that he received. Is that how Papa had found this place?

"I'm so glad that you're here," the man continued. Then he turned to me and bent forward. "And this must be your daughter."

"Yes," my father replied, pushing me forward slightly. "This is Lillian. Say hello to Herr Weidt," he added.

I curtseyed as Papa had always taught me to do whenever I was meeting someone new. "Hello, sir," I said.

The man clicked his heels together and extended his hand. "It's a pleasure to meet you, Lillian, and welcome to you as well."

"Where are we?" I blurted.

"Lillian!" There was a tone of warning in Papa's voice.

My face reddened. "Oh, pardon me," I said. "I'm not trying to be rude. Really, I'm not."

Herr Weidt smiled and brushed the comment away. "Of course not. And you must be very confused indeed. I asked your father to keep all of this a secret until you arrived. The fewer people who know about this place, the better."

Know about what? Instead of answering all my questions, this conversation was only adding to them.

"Come in," Herr Weidt finally said. "I'll show you around."

And with that, he opened a door behind him and led us into a long narrow room, humming with activity. A row of small tables, almost like the desks my friends and I had once sat behind in school, were lined up on either side of a center aisle. Men and women were seated behind these desks holding bundles of what looked like straw, or thick threads of some kind. They were weaving the fibers together and binding them into fat bunches, then scraping them across a line of nails that protruded straight up, as if they were combing the tangles out of them, just like I used to brush the knots out of my long, dark hair. Some of the workers had machines that cut the fibers down to a precise length. The machines sounded like our butcher chopping meat in the market. They made a hacking noise as the blades went up like cleavers and then slammed down onto a wooden platform. Fibers tumbled to the ground like snow falling in winter. The people were hard at work, faces pressed down to the bundles in their hands. No one looked up when we walked in.

"You must be very curious about what's happening here," Herr Weidt said, reading my mind much like the way Papa always did.

"These people work for me, and they're making brushes and brooms. That's what my factory produces," he said proudly.

I frowned. Brushes didn't impress me very much. Of course, we all used them, now and then. But what was so important about brushes? Besides, this narrow room with only a dozen or so machines didn't look much like a factory, at least not the kind I knew about. A factory was a big building with many machines.

"The army needs my products," Herr Weidt continued. "This is a very important factory for the Nazi soldiers. They need my brushes to polish shoes and clean uniforms, to brush their teeth and their hair. I don't want to support Hitler and his Nazi military, but in this factory, I can keep my workers safe."

I still wasn't sure what was so important about all of that. And I also didn't like the idea of doing anything to help the Nazis.

"There's something else you should know, Lillian," Papa interjected. "It's one of the reasons we're here. All of the workers in Herr Weidt's factory are blind, just like me."

I gasped. All the workers blind? I looked around the room again. The brush hairs were flying through the hands of the workers at their little desks. The men and women weaved the fibers in and out of their machines so fast that it was all mostly a blur. How could they do that if they couldn't see what they were doing? How did they not chop their fingers off in the process?

"Papa, you won't believe how fast everyone is working!"

"Yes, I can hear the machines," Papa replied, smiling.

"And do you know what else?" Herr Weidt asked, tapping his temple close to his eye. "I don't have much sight, myself."

My jaw dropped open. "You don't?"

"No," he replied, shaking his head.

"But you own this whole factory!"

"I started with nothing, and I built it up to what it is today," Herr Weidt said. "And there weren't many to lend me a hand."

"Just like my Papa," I whispered.

He nodded. "And now, my promise is to help other blind people, like your father."

Herr Weidt led us through the factory, pausing here and there to introduce us to the workers. I wanted to stop and talk to each one of them. But Herr Weidt pushed us along.

"There will be time to get to know each other later," he said.

We walked from table to table, shaking hands with the men and women who paused and nodded politely at me and Papa. But there was one more thing Herr Weidt told me. Not only was each person blind, but they were also all Jewish. At a time when Jewish people could not find work, Herr Weidt had given each of these people a job.

"So, you're hiring my father and the others because no one else will hire a Jewish person, especially one who's blind," I said after we had walked the length of the room.

Herr Weidt sighed. "People like your father and the others are being treated so badly these days. It's hard enough being blind, but having to deal with that kind of persecution against Jews makes my stomach churn."

My heart swelled nearly to bursting when he said that.

When the tour was over, Herr Weidt turned to us. "We'll begin your training tomorrow. But for now, you both must be exhausted and hungry."

I had lost track of the time since we had left our

home in a hurry that morning. Papa hadn't wanted to take the tram, afraid that soldiers might be inspecting the trains for Jews. So, we had walked, a distance that would normally only take a couple of hours. But we had taken a long, roundabout route, circling back every now and then when Papa thought someone might be following. Herr Weidt's words suddenly made me realize how tired I was. My head pounded and longed for a warm bed to sink into. And my stomach gurgled and called out for food.

"You need a place to stay," Herr Weidt continued. "I take care of that for all my workers, finding them homes with good people. I have just such a place for you. There's a lovely woman who lives close to my factory, a good friend of mine. She'll give you a place to sleep and food to eat. You'll be safe there."

Safe! I hadn't felt safe for so long, I realized. But now, for the first time in a long time, I was beginning to believe that I might be.

Chapter 3

Hedwig Porschütz lived about a fifteen-minute walk from the factory, near Alexanderplatz, a large public square full of shops, apartment buildings, and restaurants. Her apartment was up a flight of stairs inside a three-story brick building. A stone path led to a bright red door. Flower boxes hung under the outside windows. They were empty now in the cool fall weather. But I pictured that in spring and summer, they would overflow with white daisies and yellow daffodils, just like the flowers that had grown outside the house where we had lived in Kreuzberg. I knew those flowers were all gone as well.

Frau Porschütz opened the door after Papa knocked

and pulled us in from the hallway without even asking who we were.

"Otto told me you'd be here," she exclaimed. "It's best to get you inside quickly," she added, glancing around Papa's shoulder before closing the door. "You never know who might be watching. Not everyone is a friend, I'm afraid."

I shivered in the entranceway while she stood back to look at us.

"Herr Frey," she said, reaching out to take Papa's hand. He bowed to her. "And you must be Lillian. Welcome to both of you!"

Frau Porschütz was not much older than Papa, I thought. She was wearing a simple flowered house-dress with her hair brushed back behind her ears and held there with silver clips. She had a round face, a colored tint to her cheeks, and she was wearing bright red lipstick. When she smiled, I noticed that some of it had gotten on her front teeth. I tried not to stare.

"I'm not so fond of my first name—Hedwig." She wrinkled her nose when she said this. "So, everyone calls me Hetti, and you must call me that as well, even you, Lillian."

"No," Papa protested. "It's not proper."

Hetti waved the comment away. "I really don't care much for formality. I insist on Hetti, even from you, Herr Frey. From now on, I will call you Morris. So, it's settled then, right?"

I looked over at Papa who shrugged helplessly.

"You poor *Mäuschen*, little mouse," Hetti said, looking directly at me. "So terrible to be on the run like this."

I gulped. Hetti clapped her hands together.

"But first things first," she said. "You must be starving."

I was, though I wasn't going to say anything. Papa would have said that was rude. One had to wait to be asked. But, it had been many hours since I had eaten anything. I glanced over at Papa and then looked up at Hetti, nodding gratefully. She led us to a table in her dining room, already set with a linen tablecloth and white dishes.

"Sit, sit!" she exclaimed. "I've prepared a little something for you." With that, she disappeared into the kitchen and reappeared a moment later, carrying a platter heaped with steaming meatballs and potato dumplings. The smell was heavenly.

My eyes widened. I hadn't seen this amount of food in ages. There were strict rations on food in Berlin.

For Jews like Papa and me, it had been impossible to get much of anything to eat. But I knew that even Christian people, like Hetti, had their food allowance restricted. Where had all this come from?

"Otto helps me get food," Hetti explained, as if reading my mind. "But I also have a few connections myself." She winked when she said that.

It all sounded so mysterious, and I had no idea what it meant. But in that moment, I didn't care. There was enough food here for two families, maybe more than that! And I needed to eat.

Papa hadn't said a word since we had walked in. "Are you all right?" I asked, leaning toward him.

That was when I noticed tears glistening in his eyes. "I'm so grateful," he whispered. "Overwhelmed, really. It's been so long since anyone has been kind to us."

I reached out and took Papa's hand, squeezing it tightly. Hetti took a tissue from the sleeve of her dress and dabbed at her eyes. "You're going to make me cry as well," she said. "Don't thank me. It's Otto who is the real angel. Besides, I live alone now. My husband died some time ago, and we were never blessed with children. So, I'm also grateful for the company. Now, eat, eat," she urged, "before it gets cold." She smiled again. The lipstick smudge on her teeth was still there.

I ate two helpings of the meatballs and then devoured two slices of apple strudel that appeared out of Hetti's kitchen. I ate until there wasn't room for another bite. My head was starting to feel as heavy as my stomach, and my eyes fluttered and drooped. I needed to sleep. And once again, Hetti came to my rescue.

"Dear Mäuschen," she said. "I think I need to get you to bed."

She led us down the hallway, stopping at the first open door and indicating that Papa would be sleeping in this bedroom. He walked inside, feeling his way from the bed to the dresser to the small window, and then nodded at me and Hetti.

"I'll sleep on the couch and you, Lillian, will take my bedroom, right next door to your father," she said.

Papa started to protest, but Hetti stopped him.

"There will be no argument, Morris," she said. "I'm not much of a sleeper, and the couch is perfectly fine for me."

Then Papa turned back to me, reaching out to pull me in for a tight hug. "Will you be all right?"

I gulped. "I'll be fine."

Hetti led me into her bedroom, said good-night, and closed the door behind her. I slumped down on the bed and looked around, suddenly longing for my own bedroom in my own home in Kreuzberg. I closed my eyes and thought of my four-poster bed and the eiderdown quilt in bright ocean blue, my favorite color. My shelf had sagged from the weight of the books that Papa had bought me, books like *Hansel and Gretel*, which I loved even though it was scary when the witch in the story kidnapped the brother and sister and wanted to eat them! I had read that book so many times that the printing inside had faded, and the hard cover had become soft and bendable.

I imagined the dolls that had sat on my bed, each one in its own special place. When I opened my eyes, all of it was gone. I felt empty, even though I had just finished that big meal. *How does that happen?* I wondered. *How can I feel so empty and so full at the same time?* I knew I had to be grateful to be here with Papa, and I was! But it was hard when it felt as if everything in my life had been taken away from me.

And that's when I thought about Mama.

She had died a year ago. She and Papa had worked in the textile shop together. Each day, she went with him to the shop, helping to open it in the morning, standing behind the cash register all day while Papa sold fabric to women who came in wanting to sew a

new dress or new jacket. But then, Mama became ill
with an infection in her lungs that got worse and worse
until one day, she could no longer breathe at all.

And then she died. I was eleven years old when
that happened, and I remembered it as though it were
yesterday.

"Maybe, it's best Mama isn't here to see all these
terrible changes," Papa had said when a new decree
was announced ordering that all Jews had to turn in
their telephones and could no longer get ration cards
for clothes.

I hadn't answered. I didn't want to be here to see all
these laws either. But I didn't want Mama to die! And
I couldn't imagine that she had wanted to leave us like
that. I wanted her with me now more than ever.

I closed my eyes again and summoned up an image
of her; lips as red as Hetti's, almond-shaped eyes as
blue as cornflowers, her hair piled high on her head.
She had a way of twirling it around and around her
finger until she could form a tight bun. Then, she
would pin it to the top of her head with hairpins that
disappeared into her bun like twigs into a bird's nest.
She used as many as she could, until she was satisfied
that the bun wouldn't move. I could have watched her
twirl and pin her hair for hours.

If Papa was all strength in my life, then Mama had been all heart. She cried at everything, even when I received a good grade in school, which never made any sense to me. Crying if I failed would have been more understandable!

I choked back the tears that threatened to drown me whenever I thought of Mama. As much as I adored my father—he had been trying his hardest to be both mother and father to me—it wasn't always enough. I wiped my eyes and sat up straighter. I couldn't let myself get too sad or I wouldn't be able to face whatever was coming in the days ahead. Finally, I pulled my small suitcase up onto the bed and opened it, rummaging through the few clothing items I had managed to bring. I hadn't had much time to pack before running from our home in Kreuzberg. The warning from our neighbor that Nazi soldiers were patrolling from door to door in our neighborhood and arresting Jewish families had sent us scurrying into the streets with hardly any time to gather our things. I had hastily thrown a few skirts, sweaters, and blouses into the case with Papa pacing and begging me to hurry.

"We need to go, now!" he had said. I could tell he was trying to keep the urgency out of his voice and failing miserably. And then, at the last minute, just before I had clicked the case shut, I had placed one of my dolls on top of my pile of clothes. I pulled her from the case and held her close to me now.

I called the doll *Schatzi*, little treasure. It was what Mama had sometimes called me, as well. Schatzi's face was made of shiny porcelain with eyes of glass. Her cheeks were painted pink, and she had real hair that lay in short blonde curls around her forehead and face. Mama had made the dress that she wore. It was blue gingham with a lacy smock on top.

I ran my finger over the small dimple in her chin. "It's just you and me now, Schatzi," I said, burying my face in her hair and clutching her tightly.

Finally, I climbed into bed and pulled my doll up close. I was asleep in seconds.

Chapter 4

When I opened my eyes, sunlight was streaming into the room through the little window next to the bed. I sat up, stretched, and yawned, feeling so much more energized than the day before. I had needed that sleep more than I had thought. Papa, on the other hand, looked gaunt and his skin was gray. His eyes were ringed from lack of sleep. He muttered something to me about having too many worries on his mind. I didn't ask any questions; I didn't need to.

Hetti was not there when Papa and I went into the dining room. I read Papa the note she had left, saying she was at the market getting a few things that we might need. She had also left us a plate of soft rolls covered with a kitchen towel so they wouldn't dry out. Coffee was simmering in a pot on the stove. Hetti's note to us also added a warning at the end. "Please be careful going to the factory. The streets can be dangerous."

The feeling of a good night's sleep faded away. Nothing had changed overnight, I realized. Everything was just as unsafe as it had been the day before. Papa and I ate quickly and silently. Then, we buttoned on our coats and left Hetti's home to make our way to Herr Weidt's factory.

It felt good to be outside, breathing in the fresh air and letting the sun wash over me. Even though the sky was clear, there was a bite of cold in the air. I could see my breath when I exhaled. I tugged again on my jacket sleeves, and pulled my collar up to my neck. Then, I ducked my head, clutched Papa's arm, and tried to keep up with his long strides as we walked the few blocks to Herr Weidt's factory.

The streets were busy with people rushing to work, pushing past Papa and me, and barely looking over to see who we might be. That was just fine, as far as I was concerned. I wanted to make myself small and invisible. Thankfully, there were no soldiers in sight. Once, I looked up, startled to realize where we were. I had not paid any attention the night before. All I had wanted was to get to Hetti's house, eat, and sleep.

Now, in the bright light of the day, I realized that we were in Mitte, a district of Berlin just north of Kreuzberg, not far from the textile shop where Papa had worked. The Neue Synagogue on Oranienburger Strasse was only a ten-minute walk away. I had only been there once when Papa took me to see what the grand synagogue looked like. It was now off-limits to Jews. This whole neighborhood had once flourished with Jewish shops, cafés, and businesses that now refused to served Jewish customers. The Nazis had closed all the Jewish establishments, and Germans had taken over the businesses for themselves.

The Jewish Home for the Aged that stood on a corner just ahead of us was where elderly Jewish people were now being assembled and taken to the train station and sent to those terrible concentration camps. This home had once been a place for elderly Jewish people to live out their lives in peace. But now, it was a place that would cut Jewish lives short. I ducked my head again realizing with a heavy heart that the freedom I had once known was gone. Here, in the daylight, I felt more exposed than ever, and the walk for those few short blocks seemed endless.

Across Rosenthaler Strasse and down the narrow laneway, Papa and I finally made it to the factory door.

He knocked, and we waited for Herr Weidt to answer. He was as welcoming as he had been the night before. I still had so many questions running through my mind, questions that I hadn't been able to ask Papa. How was my father going to learn to make brushes? What would I do here in the factory? And most importantly, how were we going to remain safe when it seemed that everyone was out to get us?

The room with the brush machines was as busy as it had been the evening before. Workers were gathered in front of their small tables and were weaving and stringing brushes and brooms together. I wanted to meet some of these people. Herr Weidt had quickly introduced a few of them the day before. But, I was curious to know more. Who were they? And how had they gotten here? But, there was no chance of any conversation. Herr Weidt set to work training Papa.

"These brushes are made from horsehair," he explained, holding up a bundle that looked like thick, dark string. "First, you need to comb the hairs until all the knots are gone."

He showed Papa how to do that, pulling the hairs across those jutting nails, over and over. Once the horsehair was perfectly straight and knot-free, Herr Weidt showed Papa how to cut it to the right length for the brushes using the hacking machine, their hands doing the work. "Not too long and not too short," he explained, running the tangle-free horsehair under the cutting machine.

Finally, he showed Papa how to tie the hairs tightly together, and fix them onto the wooden bases with glue and wire, all by feeling rather than seeing. Herr Weidt stood back, holding up a brush with perfect even bristles, glued firmly and securely onto a small wooden paddle. Then, Papa walked up to the table. He was a smart student, and a quick learner. Within a short time, Herr Weidt stepped back and let Papa take over.

"Yes," he said, examining Papa's work. "I think you've got it."

And then Herr Weidt turned to me. "And now, Lillian, would you like a job in the factory as well?"

I nodded. "Oh, yes!" I had already realized that there were no young people my age who were working here. Everyone was a grown-up. "I'd really like to help."

"Good," said Herr Weidt. "Your job will be to count the brushes and help package them for shipment. This is very important work," he added. "You can read the orders that others can't see."

He led me across the room to a long table that held

about a half a dozen large boxes, piled on top of one another. Each box had an order form with the number and types of brushes that had been requested. I picked up one of the forms and silently read the order; thirty-six scrubbing brushes, twenty shoe brushes, twelve metal brushes, fifty toothbrushes. Herr Weidt told me that I would need to go to the workers and pick up their finished brushes according to what was being ordered on these forms. Then, I would fill the box with the specified products, seal it with tape, tie it with string, and move on to fill another one and another, until every request had been filled.

"If you don't know what something is, just ask one of the workers," Herr Weidt said. "I'm certain that you'll catch on in no time."

I nodded and began to walk around the room picking up brushes and carrying them back to my station. I had no trouble picking out the toothbrushes and scrubbing brushes. I wasn't sure about a couple of the other items.

"Excuse me," I said, stopping at the table of an older woman. "Can you please tell me what you're making?"

She looked up and in my direction. "Metal brushes," she replied. "The bristles are metal instead of horsehair. They're used for cleaning certain types of machinery."

I checked my order form and took a number of the finished ones to place in a box. Herr Weidt stood over me the whole time I was working. Even though he had said that he didn't have much sight, somehow he seemed to know what I was putting into each and every box. He nodded his approval.

"You're as quick a learner as your father is," he exclaimed. "I was right to bring both of you into my factory. I'm lucky to have you here."

Papa raised his head from the work he was doing at his desk. He had moved on from gluing brushes to cutting straw for brooms. "We're the lucky ones," Papa said. "We're so grateful you're allowing us to work here."

Herr Weidt clapped him on the back. "You don't need to thank me. I'm doing what any decent citizen of this country should be doing. Besides," he added, "making brushes requires a special touch. *Feeling* the brush is more important than *seeing* what you're doing."

I was pretty sure that people who could see would also be able to make brushes! But, I was thankful that Herr Weidt had taken us in.

Papa and I worked side by side all morning. The time passed quickly, and before I knew it, Herr Weidt was calling for all the workers to take a break.

Finally! I thought. *A chance to meet some of the other people.* Papa and I sat together at a table in the back of the room, and pulled out the sandwiches that Hetti had also left for us. A young woman sat next to me.

"Hello," I said.

She looked up from the sandwich that she was eating. The crease in her forehead deepened as she stared at me, noticeably uncomfortable.

"Who are you?" she asked, a bit of tightness in her voice.

"I'm Lillian Frey. I'm here with my father. We arrived yesterday."

I could see some of the caution melt away from this woman. Her shoulders relaxed and she reached out her hand to shake mine.

"Sorry," she said. "I'm so used to being suspicious whenever a stranger speaks to me. Pleased to meet you, Lillian. I'm Anneliese Bernstein. I'm here with my sister."

Anneliese looked as if she was in her twenties. I could see that she wasn't blind, and I was trying to figure out a way to ask her about that. I'd been told that Herr Weidt employed *only* blind people at his workshop. But just then, another young woman sat down next to Anneliese. I gasped when I saw the two of them next to one another.

"You're twins!" I blurted. The resemblance was startling, the same dark, curly hair framing big, green eyes and wide smiles with a deep dimple on each cheek.

Anneliese grinned. "Identical in every way. This is my sister, Marianne."

"Well, not quite every way," Marianne said, reaching out to shake my hand as well. "I'm the one of the two of us who is blind. I had an infection when I was a child that caused the nerves in my eyes to swell. We're here because of me."

Anneliese explained that they had been here for six months. She had once worked as a dressmaker in Berlin. But eventually, that was no longer possible. "No one would bring their dresses to a Jew," she explained, "even though I could shorten a hem or redesign a blouse better than most other dressmakers." That was when she and her sister had sought refuge here, where Herr Weidt had trained both of them to make brushes.

"He's our angel," Anneliese said.

Marianne nodded and gestured around the table where other workers had stopped eating to listen in on our conversation. "Everyone will agree with me."

She went on to introduce several of the other workers. There was Willy Latter who had been blind since he was my age, after doctors had botched the eye surgery that was meant to correct a small problem. He had been working here for a year. Bernhard Bromberger became blind after an eye infection when he was a young man. Erna Haney was the woman I had asked about the metal brushes. She had been blind from birth and had arrived just about a week before Papa and me.

Each person had a story about where they had come from, how they had become blind, and how Herr Weidt had taken them in and saved them from a terrible fate.

"He's saved all of us," Erna said, insisting that I also call her by her first name.

"An angel," Herr Bromberger added, echoing Anneliese.

I was beginning to realize how true that was.

Chapter 5

We continued working once the lunch break was over. But now, there seemed to be a feeling of ease in the air that hadn't been there before. It was as if by introducing ourselves and eating together, we had broken the ice with the other workers. They now knew Papa and me by name. They were less quiet, less suspicious—more friendly.

"I still remember seeing a sunset even though I've been blind for so many years," Herr Bromberger said, as I stood watching him weave bundles of fibers together to make a broom. He had silver hair and a film of some kind over his eyes that made them look glossy. "It was so red, it was like watching a fire on the horizon," he said. "I remember that color so well."

"I remember a sun so yellow it looked like the yolk of an egg," added Marianne. "And I can remember what eggs looked like."

Willy Latter was quiet. The deep worry lines on his face told the story of a difficult life. He had been a concert pianist and music teacher. His wife and two daughters were in hiding somewhere outside of Berlin. He didn't know where they were and hadn't been with them for some time.

Erna Haney sighed. "I wish I could have seen a sunset or an egg." I remembered that she had been born blind. She suddenly looked nervous. "My husband isn't Jewish," she said, lowering her voice. "I thought that would protect me from being targeted by the Nazis. But I was wrong. There is no protection."

My throat tightened. Erna must have sensed me stiffen. "But we're safe here, my dear," she said. "I don't want you to worry about that." She paused and then added. "My husband managed to get our two boys out of the country. I'm so happy about that. But I miss them every minute of every day."

My mind jumped to thoughts of Mama. I missed her every day as well.

The day passed quickly. I packed boxes of supplies. Papa and the other workers cut, combed, and assembled brushes and brooms. In between, we talked about our lives and what we missed. I had to admit, the work was fun, and working side by side with Papa was something I had never done before. Still, all the talk about leaving things behind made me miss my home as well. As grateful as I was to Herr Weidt, life wasn't the same as it had been before all the troubles. And it wasn't the same being the only young person in the middle of all these grown-ups. I missed my friends.

I hadn't seen my best friend, Ruth, for many months. I had no idea where she was or if she was safe. We hadn't met until my family fled to Berlin, but it was as if we had known each other our entire lives. Her family was among the few Jewish families in our Kreuzberg neighborhood, and we became inseparable. We lived next door to each other and walked to and from school together. In class, we sat next to one another. We wore the same ribbons in our hair that we braided in the same style. We could almost finish each other's sentences. And because neither of us had siblings, we had always pretended that we were sisters.

We planned to grow up and live next door to each other forever. A trapdoor of memories swung open as I summoned up one of our conversations.

"Show me the painting you made in school," Ruth *said as we walked home one afternoon.*

I hesitated. "It's so bad. You know I can't draw."

"Show me," she insisted.

I pulled the drawing from my bag and held it up to her. She studied it for a long time, her head tilting first to the right, and then to the left.

"It's not…terrible," she finally said. "That tree looks pretty good." She pointed to one side of my drawing.

I paused and then said, "That's not a tree. It's a man."

Another long pause. "Oh."

We looked at one another, and a second later, we exploded with laughter.

"It feels as if you're a million miles away from me, my darling child." Papa's voice interrupted my thoughts as I passed by his workstation. And once again, it amazed me that he could sense what I was thinking and feeling, even though he couldn't see my face. It was as if the feelings in my body oozed out of me and into the air where Papa would catch them and understand them.

"I was thinking about Ruth," I replied, always honest

with Papa. "And I've been thinking about Mama," I added, dropping my voice until it was really just a whisper.

Papa stopped pulling horsehair into a tight bundle. "I know you miss them," he said.

"Yes," I replied.

"I miss your Mama as well. But she would want us to look to the future," he added. "To focus on getting through the days to come. I'm sure your friend Ruth would want the same."

"But do you think she's safe? Ruth, I mean."

"I pray every day that she and all of our friends are out of harm's way," Papa replied.

"I pray that for my friends and family as well," added Herr Bromberger, who had been listening to our conversation.

"And my friends and family," said Marianne.

"And mine," echoed Willy Latter.

"And my children," said Erna.

Tears pooled in my eyes as I looked around the room, blinking rapidly. Every single person here had friends and family members who were somewhere out there.

I wasn't the only one who worried about loved ones.

Chapter 6

Herr Weidt disappeared after lunch, but he returned
to the factory near the end of the day.

"Business meetings," he said vaguely as he came to
stand next to me. I was in the middle of packing a large
order of supplies and struggling to close the lid of the
box. He stepped in to help me tape it shut and wrap
it with string.

"Tell me how you are doing, Lillian," he said as we
pushed the sealed box aside and I moved on to filling
another one with shoe brushes.

"I'm fine, thank you, Herr Weidt," I replied.

"And did you sleep well last night? Did Hetti look
after you?"

"Oh, yes. She's very nice. And very kind."

"I'm glad to hear that," Herr Weidt replied. "I want you to feel safe here."

I lowered my head and bit my lower lip, not knowing how to respond. I didn't want to tell Herr Weidt about my longing for Mama and my worries about Ruth. That might make him think I was ungrateful for all he was doing to help us.

"Yes, I understand," Herr Weidt finally said, when seconds of silence had passed. "Nothing feels very safe right now."

I looked up. He was reading my mind, just like Papa. Finally, he sighed deeply and turned to Papa.

"I'd like the two of you to follow me to the back of the factory. There's something that I need to show you. Something that's also for your safety," he added, looking right at me.

Papa stopped what he was doing, put the bristles back down on his small table, and together we followed Herr Weidt.

At the back of the workshop was a door. It looked like the door to a wardrobe of some kind. We stood and watched Herr Weidt open it. Inside were several coats and smocks hanging on coat hangers. I took a step closer, curious as to why Herr Weidt had brought us over here and what this had to do with our protection.

"I've told you that you're safe here, and you are," he began. "But out there," he gestured toward the street, "out there, it's a different story. And I'm afraid that the Gestapo is searching everywhere for Jews, even here in my little factory."

A cold chill passed up and down my spine. I already knew what the streets of Berlin were like. But Herr Weidt and all the others had told us that we would be out of harm's way here, inside the factory. Now, he was talking about soldiers coming to search for us inside this place. And I knew what the Gestapo was. This secret police unit of the Nazi army was responsible for searching for Jews who might be hiding in places just like this one.

"But I have a plan for that," Herr Weidt continued.

And then, to my surprise, he lifted one foot, stepped into the wardrobe, and disappeared inside. I leaned forward and watched as he moved past the coats and smocks that were hanging on the rod and pressed against the back wall. It clicked open, and he pushed this concealed door wide open, turning to beckon to me and my father. "Help your father through this door," he instructed.

"Papa, take my arm," I said. I pushed my father's head down and nudged him forward, helping him to climb into the wardrobe, past the hanging garments, through the open back door, and emerging a moment later into another room. Herr Weidt was waiting for us on the other side.

"I had no idea this room was here," I exclaimed as I looked around. The room was small, perhaps only ten feet long and ten feet wide. There was nothing inside, no chairs, no tables, and no windows to the outside world. One lightbulb was suspended from the ceiling, and it cast a pale glow across the room.

"That's the idea," said Herr Weidt, smiling from ear to ear. "You didn't know it was here, and the Gestapo doesn't know it's here."

He went on to tell us that, from time to time, soldiers conducted raids on his factory. "I believe it's intended as a drill," he added as I caught my breath. "They want to remind us of the power they have. So, they come through factories like mine to make sure we're following their rules."

To make sure there are no Jewish workers here, I thought.

"We can't take any chances," Herr Weidt continued. "I always have one of my trusted friends posted at the front door of the factory. If there's any danger at all, if my friend sees that a Nazi patrol is approaching, he'll ring the bell downstairs and you'll hear it in the factory. That's the signal to immediately stop what you're doing and come back here. All of you," he added. "You will all climb through that wardrobe and into this room. And you'll stay here, not moving, and not making a sound, until someone comes to tell you that the danger has passed. Then you can come out again."

I didn't like the sound of this one bit. Herr Weidt said that his hidden room was for our protection, and I could see that it had been set up for that reason. But I felt as if our lives were in more danger than ever. It was unnerving; one minute hearing the promise of safety, the next minute fearing a Nazi patrol's approach.

"It's very important that you understand this plan and that you follow my directions," Herr Weidt said. He turned to me. "I'll be counting on you to help your father and the others get into this secret room."

Up until now, Papa had not said a word. But now, he placed one arm protectively around my shoulder. And then he stepped forward and reached out to grasp Herr Weidt's hand.

"We will do whatever you ask of us," he said.

Chapter 7

After having crawled through the little wardrobe and into the safe room at the back of Herr Weidt's factory, I couldn't shake the feeling of dread that sat in my body.

That night, I dreamed I was in a dark tunnel.

Someone was shouting at me to move forward as quickly as I could. Don't stop! Don't look back! a voice commanded. I crept forward, slithering like a snake while coats and jackets and apron strings brushed past my face like the long, tangled vines hanging from a tall tree. Where was Papa? Where were Herr Weidt and the other workers? A choked cry rose up in my throat along with the bitter taste of bile. I thought I might be sick. The tunnel was endless—no light, no air, my eyes straining to see some shapes. Something was chasing me. I heard loud, angry voices and saw the glint of a soldier's rifle behind me. This would be the end of Papa and me.

I must have cried out in my sleep because suddenly someone was shaking my shoulder. I opened my eyes to see Papa standing over me.

"My darling," he cried. "I'm here. I'm with you."

I sat up in bed, shaking from head to toe and trying desperately to still the wild beating of my heart. Papa placed his hand, so cool, on my hot forehead, streaked with sweat.

"Can you tell me what it was?" he asked, sinking onto my bed and holding my hand.

"A dream."

"More like a nightmare, I think," Papa said.

"Yes." My voice felt as shaky as my body.

"Would you like to tell me about it?"

I hesitated at first. I didn't want to worry Papa any more than he already was. He had always protected *me*, but I now felt responsible for *him* as well. Besides, here in the quiet of Hetti's house, it seemed silly that I should be dreaming about tunnels and crawling and getting away from the police. None of it was real.

"Sometimes it's better when you talk and get your worries out in the open," Papa urged.

I hesitated a moment longer, and then began to tell

him everything. He listened patiently, nodding and clucking sympathetically when I described my dream. I told him the soldiers had been so close I could almost feel them breathing at my neck. He held my hand and sat with me until my heart stopped hammering, my body stopped trembling, and there was nothing more to tell.

"Do you think things will ever get back to normal?" I finally asked. It was something I hadn't asked my father before. I sensed that he wouldn't know the answer. Or perhaps I was afraid that he would, and it wouldn't be something I wanted to hear.

Papa sighed. "Best not to think about that, my darling. Let's just try to remember how lucky we are to be here and protected by Otto Weidt."

Protected! In the past, protected had meant sleeping in my own bed, in my own house, with both of my parents in the next room. Now, it meant sneaking through the streets of Berlin to a factory that had a secret room in the back to hide in!

"Do you think you can sleep now?" Papa asked.

"I'll try."

"I'm right next door if you need me. I'm always close by."

I lay back down on my pillow as Papa pulled the

blankets up to my neck. He kissed me on the forehead and left the room. When he was gone, I reached for Schatzi, finding my doll buried in a tangle of sheets next to me. I pulled her up close to me, but my body still twitched with anxiety, and I couldn't let it go. Then, I held my doll at arm's length, staring in the dark at her features. *She's no help at all*, I thought. *She can't comfort me or make the fears go away. She's just a hollow, porcelain doll with a painted happy smile.* Angrily, I threw her away from me. But a moment later, I reached for her and cradled her against me once more. That's when I finally fell asleep.

Chapter 8

A few days later, Papa and I returned to Hetti's home after a long day at the factory to find a surprise waiting for me. In the days in between, I had tried to push the images of the factory being searched out of my head. While at work, I would glance, every now and then, at the back of the factory and the wardrobe concealing the secret room. But then, I would look quickly away, and return to boxing the orders. Once, Herr Weidt caught me looking to the back.

"I'm afraid I scared you by showing you the secret room. I didn't mean to do that. Having that room back there is a way to protect you."

"I know it's important," I said.

"My workers are all grown-ups," he said, sweeping his arm across the factory room. "I forget that you're still a young girl. Children shouldn't have to worry about these things."

I nodded. "But I do. And I worry about my Papa and how he'll manage if we ever have to hide back there."

"He'll manage," Herr Weidt replied. "And you'll help him. And so will the others. We're all here to help each other. Don't forget that."

That conversation stayed with me as we walked into Hetti's apartment and closed the door behind us.

"Come in, come in, Mäuschen, and see what I've got for you," said Hetti. We barely had a chance to remove our coats. She was practically dancing on the spot, shifting from one foot to the other, and urging Papa and me to go into the dining room. There, on her dining room table was a cake. And in the center of it was a candle burning brightly in the dim light of the room.

"Happy birthday!" shouted Hetti, grinning from ear to ear.

I startled and turned to her, mouth open, eyes widening.

"Your father told me," Hetti continued. "I told him

not to say a word all day and to wait until the two of you were back here for the surprise."

"You have no idea how much I wanted to say something," Papa added.

"I couldn't let a birthday go by without a small party," Hetti continued. "Even in these times, every child needs to have a birthday!"

My birthday! I had completely forgotten about it. After Mama died, my birthday had become less special. Mama had been the one to prepare a cake and buy a present. Papa tried after she was gone, but it wasn't the same. Still, it had never passed without some kind of celebration, even a small one.

How was it possible that this year I had forgotten, when for my whole life I had always looked forward to my birthday? And yet, in the midst of everything that was happening around us, my birthday had disappeared from my mind, like snow melting from the ground in winter.

"It isn't much," Hetti added, pushing me forward. "Go ahead, Mäuschen. Make a wish and blow out the candle."

What to wish for? I stared at the cake and the candle growing shorter with each passing second. Finally, I closed my eyes and whispered, "Keep Papa and me safe. And Ruth as well." Then I opened my eyes and blew the candle out.

Papa had one more surprise for me. "I brought this with us when we left the house. I knew I'd give it to you at some point. Now, I think, is a good time."

He pulled something from his jacket pocket and dropped it into my hand. When I looked down, I gasped. There, in my palm, was a small brooch shaped like a cornflower, the flower of Germany. It had been Mama's favorite flower, and Papa had given her this pin on one of her birthdays. It had a ring of deep blue-violet flower heads clustered around a darker center. It sat on a solid gold base.

"Like the blue of her eyes," Papa said.

"I love it." I looked up at him, tears pooling in my eyes.

"I knew you would," Papa replied.

Then, I turned to Hetti. "And thank you for this cake. It makes me happy, and it's more than I ever imagined."

She sniveled and dabbed at her eyes. "Come. That's enough crying for one night. Today is a celebration. Let's eat."

Chapter 9

"Cornflowers," said Marianne, sighing deeply when I told her and the other workers about the brooch Papa had given me. "They're my favorite as well."

"You're lucky to have something so precious," Erna added when I had described the pin in detail for her and the others who couldn't see the blue stones of the flower on the gold backing.

I even showed it to Herr Weidt. He reached out to touch it, running his fingers over it so he could feel what it looked like.

"It must mean so much to you," he said.

I swallowed, not able to say a word.

I wore the pin to the factory that day, and the next one, and the one after that. I vowed that I wouldn't ever take it off; it was that special to me. And more than anything else, it was a reminder of Mama. It was as if I was carrying her with me on the collar of my blouse or my sweater. All I had to do was reach up, touch the pin, and Mama's face would flash before my eyes. Somehow, everything felt better knowing that a part of her was with me.

As the weeks went by, Papa and I fell into our new routine. We rose at dawn, ate the rolls, and drank the coffee that Hetti had prepared. Then, we walked the few blocks to the factory. I always kept my head down and clutched Papa's arm for both our sakes. He needed my sight and I needed his encouragement.

Winter had descended on the city and snow blanketed the ground. The air was bitterly cold when Papa and I left for work in the morning, and even chillier when we returned in the evening. Hetti had miraculously found a pair of boots for me that fit perfectly. She had even managed to find me a new winter coat, one with sleeves that were just the right length. When I asked her where she had found it, she shrugged the question away.

"It belonged to a friend of a friend who was going to throw it away. She was happy to give it to me and didn't ask any questions. And I'm happy to give it to you. I knew it would fit you like a glove."

I hugged her tightly when she said that.

Every day, I packed boxes in the factory until it was time for a lunch break. Then, I sat with Papa and the other workers eating the sandwiches that Hetti had prepared for us. After lunch, I worked at packing again. Then, Papa and I went back to Hetti's in the evening.

The days blended, one into the other. The routine became so familiar that I almost couldn't remember a time when my life had been any different. It was amazing what passing time did. It made old memories fade and replaced them with something new. Every now and then, I thought about Ruth and worried about where she was and whether or not she was safe. But then, as Papa had instructed, I tried to look ahead and focus on getting through each day.

In the evenings, we sat with Hetti listening to music on the radio that she kept in her sitting room. Hetti loved listening to opera, and she would turn up the volume when her favorite arias came on. Opera was not something that I had spent a lot of time listening to.

"So beautiful!" Hetti said one night as we sat listening. She had to raise her voice to be heard over the sound that was blasting through the sitting room.

I stifled a giggle. This wasn't beautiful as far as I was concerned. The high soprano notes of the woman singer reminded me of the squeal of train wheels as a train pulled into the station.

"You must try to feel the beautiful music and understand its sad tale," Hetti said, patiently explaining the plot to me.

It didn't help much. Every story sounded the same. There was a young woman in love with a man, but unable to find him, or meet him, or stay with him because something or someone always got in the way. Sometimes, the opera ended happily for the couple. But just as often, it ended in tragedy, one or both dying just before they found each other again. I tried to sit still and listen politely to the voices so that Hetti wouldn't be hurt. It wasn't easy.

Every now and then, a news report broke into the music. That was when the three of us would sit up, lean closer to the radio, and pay attention. The news was more tragic than the operas. One night, the broadcaster said that all Jewish people from the town of Coesfeld in northern Germany were being ordered to move to Riga, Latvia, into a walled part of that city. It was called a *ghetto*, Papa explained grimly.

"Just another kind of prison," he said.

Similar ghettos had already been built in other cities across Europe into which Jews were ordered to move. When those news items were broadcast, I longed for the opera to return to the air. I would rather listen to squealing train wheels than those scary reports.

One day, I was working in the factory, packing my boxes as usual, when Herr Weidt suddenly appeared carrying large piles of blankets and shoes and sweaters and other pieces of clothing.

"I have a new job for you, Lillian," he said, struggling under the weight of all of these items.

I rushed over to help him. "What are these for?" I asked.

He paused before answering. "You've heard about the Nazis' concentration camps, haven't you?"

I nodded and shuddered. Concentration camps were far worse than ghettos. Those were the places far away where Jewish people and others were being imprisoned, tortured, and killed.

"I've been trying to figure out how I can help those poor people, some of whom I know, who have been sent away to the camps," Herr Weidt continued. "And then it came to me. I'm going to send supplies to them." He placed his hand on top of the items. "They probably need clothing and blankets. I've heard that they weren't able to take much with them when they were rounded up and sent to the camps. And I've heard the conditions there are terrible; little food, no medicine, no warm winter clothing. I'm hoping these packages will get through to them."

I gazed at Herr Weidt. His kindness was beyond anything I had ever encountered. I was struggling to find a way to say this, but he had already begun to separate the items into piles.

"Clothing here, blankets there," he muttered. "And try to sort out the clothing items into separate stacks for men and women."

I nodded and reached for some of the sweaters and trousers, placing them inside a box that Herr Weidt had prepared. The address on the box read *Theresienstadt.* It was one of the concentration camps that Papa had talked about. Seeing the name spelled out on the box made my mouth go dry.

"Where did you find all of this?" I asked as I finished loading up one box and moved to another. The clothing was secondhand but in good condition.

He paused and turned his head away. "I'm not the only one who wants to help Jews," he said. "My friends were very generous when I put out the word that I was looking for these things."

I picked up a jacket, so small it could have fit my doll, Schatzi. Children! Babies! It was the first time I realized that there were young boys and girls among those who were being sent away. What had these Jewish children done to deserve being sent to those terrible prisons?

"Those poor souls who have been taken to the camps probably won't last long," Herr Weidt said, as we closed the last of the boxes and taped and tied it shut. "But I hope these things will make their last days more bearable."

Chapter 10

That evening, Papa and I walked home from the factory in silence. The image of the little jacket was still there in my mind, refusing to leave as if it were stuck inside.

"What is it, my darling?" Papa asked.

I smiled sadly. "You always know when something is bothering me, don't you?"

"That's what fathers are for. It's my job to know."

The streets were busy with people rushing past. A little boy ran right by us, pushing past Papa and making him stumble.

"I'm fine," Papa protested as I reached out to stop his fall. Papa was so proud; he hated having anyone look after him. He always insisted that he could do everything on his own.

"I'm fine," he repeated and continued walking. "Now, tell me why you're so troubled."

I took a deep breath and began to tell Papa about the little jacket and all the clothes that I had helped Herr Weidt pack up.

"Children are in those concentration camps, too," I whispered. "Even babies."

"Yes," Papa replied. His voice sounded as sad as I felt.

"But why do the Nazis hate the children? They haven't done anything wrong. No one has. But little children! It doesn't…"

"It doesn't make sense," Papa finished my sentence.

And then, we walked in silence once more. Nothing could explain what was happening in the world or why Jewish people were so hated.

A conversation with Ruth played through my mind, a memory of another time.

"Did you hear what Leon said to me in the play-ground?" Ruth asked one day, as we lined up to go inside the school building.

"No." I glanced around. Leon was a boy a grade ahead of us. We never mingled with the older kids, and they never paid much attention to us.

"He pushed me—hard! I waited for him to say he was

sorry. But, instead, he said, 'Watch where you're going,' as though it were my fault. And then, he screamed, 'Jew!' really loud, like it was a dirty word."

"Are you sure he meant it? Maybe it was just an accident."

"It was no accident. He sounded like he hated me, hated all of us!"

The light was fading. Streetlamps were beginning to light up, casting dusky shadows across the pavement. My breath, when I exhaled, hung in the air like an icy cloud. Snow began to fall in fat flakes that clumped together and settled on top of each other. I wanted to get home quickly. I hoped Hetti would have hot tea or, better yet, hot soup waiting for us. It was probably selfish of me to wish for food when the Jews who were in concentration camps had nothing.

We were close to Alexanderplatz. One more block, and we'd arrive at Hetti's apartment. But, as we turned the last corner, a truck suddenly pulled up, revving its motor and then squealing to a stop right in front of us. I froze and yanked on Papa's arm as two police officers got out of the truck.

"What—"

"Shhh, Papa!" I whispered. "Police!"

Papa sucked in his breath, and his face went white as ash. He pulled me against him and wrapped his arm around my shoulder.

My mind raced. Were the Gestapo police coming to arrest us? How did they know we were Jews? How could we get away? I reached up and touched my cornflower pin. Mama! But she wasn't here. Only Papa and me. And now, it was over for us.

I couldn't breathe. My chest was tight as if something was squeezing the air from my lungs. My head felt light. My arms shook. Papa held me tighter.

The Gestapo marched toward us, faces grim, eyes narrow and angry. They were only steps away. Cold prickles traveled up and down my spine as I braced myself for what was to come. But instead of stopping in front of us, instead of arresting us, instead of ordering us into the truck, the police officers marched right past and stopped in front of a building just behind us. They pounded on the door and seconds later, an elderly man answered. He had a long beard, and an embroidered skullcap was perched on his head. I knew instantly that he was an observant Jewish man.

His eyes widened when he saw the police on his doorstep. "Yes?" His voice was raspy.

"You're to come with us," one of the officers said.

"But why? I've done nothing."

"You're a Jew," the second officer interrupted. "We're cleaning the city of Jews, one by one."

I thought I might be sick as Papa clutched me even harder. By now, a crowd had gathered. Men on their way home from work, women carrying baskets of groceries, children riding their bicycles, all stopped to stare at the scene in front of us.

"But…but can I get…can I just get my coat? My hat?" he begged.

"You won't need them where you're going."

And then, the police officers stepped forward and grabbed the man, one on either side, and pulled him from the doorway, past the spot where Papa and I were standing. The man's feet dragged along the pavement and his head dropped forward.

"I've done nothing wrong!" he sobbed as the officers lifted him up into the back of the truck.

His skullcap flew from his head, floated for a moment in the icy air, and then dropped to the ground. That was when the man cried out as if someone had struck him. And then, the truck drove off.

At first, no one moved. Then slowly, the crowd began to disperse. And finally, it was just Papa and me, standing under a streetlamp, shadows deepening, light fading. My body still shook. Papa looked as if he'd seen a ghost.

"We have to go," he finally said, taking a shaky step forward.

I found my voice. "No, Papa. That's the wrong way."

We had turned around toward the terrible commotion. And now, my father, always so sure of his step, had become confused and disoriented. He stopped and twisted his head, first in one direction and then the other.

"I don't know…I don't know which way…." His voice trailed off weakly.

My head was pounding. But now it was my turn to take care of him. "It's okay, Papa," I said. "I know. Take my arm."

And with that, my proud father reached for me and held on with all his might. I glanced back over my shoulder. The old man's skullcap lay on the ground. Snow continued to fall in thick clumps, covering it until it could no longer be seen.

Chapter 11

After that evening, Papa and I walked to and from the factory even more quickly than before, heads down, saying nothing. Each car that belched smoke, every cat that meowed, each parent that shouted to their child—every sound made me jump. My eyes darted this way and that, always on the lookout for police who might be on the lookout for us. To make matters worse, Papa had become more anxious than I had ever seen him, as if the incident with the police and losing his sense of direction had unnerved him completely. The weight of having to look out for him increased with each passing day.

It was only after we arrived at the factory that Papa would take a deep breath and smile. "Herr Weidt is keeping us safe here in his workshop for the blind, just like I said he would," Papa would say to me as he took his familiar position at his workstation and began to assemble his brushes.

I longed to depend on Papa again. I wanted to trust him and to believe we would remain safe. I thought fleetingly of the snow globe that Mama and Papa had given me for my eighth birthday. I had left it behind with all of my other belongings. Inside the glass sphere was a small porcelain statue of the Eiffel Tower in Paris. I had seen pictures of it in a book; steel pillars and cables that wove together to rise up into a pointed steeple. The Eiffel Tower in my snow globe was submerged in water and surrounded by small white particles. When I shook the sphere, the particles were churned up. And they rose to the top of the globe and then floated to the bottom like flakes of snow. Nothing could touch the tower or the snowflakes. They were protected by the glass and by the water. That's what I hoped for Papa and me and the others. I wanted to pretend that all of us in Herr Weidt's factory were in a kind of bubble where nothing bad could touch us.

One day, I realized that we had been at the factory for nearly six months. And aside from a couple of scary moments, nothing bad had happened to us, just as

Papa had promised. Out there, the world was spiraling into a black hole. But here in Herr Weidt's factory, we were protected from the outside world. We were in our very own snow globe.

I was packaging a large order one day when Anneliese walked by and nudged me.

"It looks as if you're busy," she said.

"This is one of the biggest orders ever," I replied, struggling to move one of the boxes. "It'll take at least four boxes to fit everything that the military has asked for this time. I don't know what the Nazis do with all these brooms and brushes, but I'm glad they keep ordering them."

Anneliese nodded. "That's what keeps us working here. I have such mixed feelings about it. On the one hand, we're making supplies for the Nazis. For the *Nazis!*" she repeated, emphasizing the word. "I mean, they're the enemy! And yet, without their orders, we wouldn't have a job here and we'd be as helpless as all the other Jews in Berlin." She shook her head from side to side. "It's a dilemma, for sure!"

"I know what you mean," I agreed. "And I know that Herr Weidt hates the Nazis as much as we do. He tells us that all the time. But we still have to fill these orders."

"Right. No brushes, no factory. And no factory, no…us!" She shook her head again. "But, that's not what I came over here to talk to you about. I have a gift for you."

A gift? My birthday had been months ago, and I really hadn't told anyone at the factory about it, except to talk about Mama's cornflower brooch, which I continued to wear every day.

"My sister and I are living with a woman who happens to have a sewing machine in her home. She lets me use it from time to time," Anneliese said wistfully.

"Do you miss the work that you used to do?" I asked.

"Very much," Anneliese replied. "It was not only something I did for money, it was something I loved doing. It was my profession *and* my pastime."

Anneliese shook her head a third time. "I took a dress of mine that I couldn't wear any longer, and I sewed it into something that I think would be lovely for you."

She handed me a small package wrapped in brown paper and tied with string. I unwrapped it and pulled out a dress, holding it up to the light. It was the deepest shade of green with slim gold threads woven into the fabric, with matching gold buttons. They caught the light and sparkled. I pulled the dress close to me, speechless.

"It's not brand new," Anneliese explained. "But I wore the dress only once. And since I've redesigned and resized it for you, it's practically new. I hope you can wear it now. Every young girl should have a new dress from time to time, don't you think?"

I hadn't had a new dress in so long, not since Papa had brought one home for me after Mama died. I knew Papa couldn't see it, or me in it. And I didn't have the heart to tell him that the dress hung past my knees, and the sleeves draped below my wrists. "It's perfect, Papa," I had said as he beamed. This one looked as if it would fit me just right.

I blinked rapidly and looked over at Anneliese. "It's beautiful," I whispered, finding my voice. "Thank you!"

Anneliese looked away, shyly. "Good, good. Well, I just wanted you to have that." She was blinking and rubbing her eyes. "Okay, then, back to work."

With that, she moved on, leaving me standing there, still holding the dress in my hands. As I returned to my work, I marveled at our little community of Jews in Herr Weidt's factory. We were all on the run for our lives. We were all living in dangerous times. We were all uncertain of our future. And still, we could care for one another and be generous and kind.

Chapter 12

I wore the dress the very next day. And when I passed Anneliese at her workstation, she looked up. Her eyes lit up, and a huge smile spread across her face. It was as if I had given her a gift and not the other way around!

"It fits me perfectly," I said as I twirled in a circle, letting the golden threads catch the light. "You haven't lost your touch."

Anneliese reached out to grab my hand. "That's the nicest thing anyone could say to me."

I returned to my spot and began to pack up the orders for that day. Papa was working close to me. I marveled at how quick he had become in making his brushes, as if he had been born doing this work.

He looked up from his table, sensing that I had been

watching him. "Would you like to give it a try?" he asked.

It was exactly what I had been wanting to do. I moved over next to Papa and took handfuls of bristles, pressing them together as firmly as I could. Papa reached over to run his fingers lightly over the bundle that I held in my hands.

"No, Lillian," he said, shaking his head from side to side and pursing his lips. "You're going to have to twist those bristles much more tightly. Otherwise, the brush will be too soft and it'll fall apart before you know it. We can't have that happening." He took the horsehair from my hand and, with a quick twist of his wrist, bundled the fibers into a tight bale. "There, that's much better, isn't it?"

"I don't know how you can do that," I said, examining the tightly bound roll of bristles.

Papa smiled. "It's what I've always told you," he said. "Some people think being blind is an obstacle. I think…"

"I know," I interrupted. "You think it's an opportunity to learn new things." I echoed the message that my father had been telling me for years.

"That's exactly right," he said, grinning at me.

I was just about to leave the brushmaking to my

father and return to my packaging, when suddenly the bell above the door began to ring, jingling and echoing through the factory room with a persistent and relentless refrain, like the chorus of one of Hetti's operas, but much more sinister.

Everyone stopped working immediately. Silence fell on the factory floor as if night had suddenly fallen on the city.

Like everyone else, I froze, my feet glued to the floor, my hands held mid-air as I was about to pack a new box of brushes. It was the warning bell. The Nazis were here!

It was Anneliese who spoke first, calling out urgently, "Everyone, to the back. I'll lead the way."

The workers left their posts and walked to the back of the factory and to the wardrobe that concealed the hiding room.

I turned to Papa. "Take my arm," I said forcefully. "We have to move quickly!"

Papa grabbed my arm and I led him to the back. All the while, Anneliese's voice rose above the sound of footsteps shuffling across the factory floor. "Move as fast as you can," she called out. "Try not to push."

Papa and I were at the back of the group. Up ahead, there was a snarl of factory workers trying to get through the wardrobe door. I glanced over my shoulder. How long did we have? The soldiers would appear any moment. They would burst through the door and we would be doomed. My heart raced, my brain felt as if it was on fire, and panic washed over me in waves.

"One at a time. Hand on the shoulder of the person in front of you," Anneliese ordered with the voice of someone in charge. She had clearly done this before and knew what the blind workers had to do to find their way to the room behind the wardrobe. But the progress was slow and the line stalled.

"Why aren't we moving?" Papa asked, gripping my arm.

"We're just waiting for the others to get through." Though I was trying desperately to stop trembling, my voice shook. I didn't want Papa to hear how scared I was.

I was sure I could hear footsteps on the stairs. I squeezed my eyes shut, and then opened them. *Please move*, I thought desperately.

Suddenly, the path seemed to clear as the workers ahead of us passed through the hidden compartment. Papa and I were finally close to the opening. But just as we were about to step toward the door, Papa suddenly caught his foot on a loose floorboard and tumbled down with a loud thud.

"Ahhh!" he yelled.

"Papa!" I reached down to grab him under his arms, terrified that he might be badly hurt, and equally terrified that we would be found by the Nazis like this. "Get up!" My voice was hoarse with fear. Papa's eyes fluttered back in his head, and for a moment I thought he might have fainted.

"Papa!" I shouted again. The warning bell was ringing with a persistent clang. The soldiers were about to break through the door.

"Papa!" I yelled a third time.

"Yes, yes," he finally said. "I'm...I'm fine." His voice was weak and breathless.

I pulled him with all my might as Papa raised himself to one knee, trying to stand.

Boots on the staircase, clomping closer and closer.

Loud voices.

Papa struggling.

I pulled again, trying to take his weight into my arms.

And then, Anneliese appeared from the other side of the wardrobe.

She instantly sized up the situation and grabbed Papa on one side, while I moved to the other.

"Pull!" she commanded.

Together, we tugged and finally raised Papa from the floor. There was a welt on the side of his cheek where he must have struck his face. We had run out of time and had to get through the door.

Anneliese jumped into the wardrobe first, and then turned to pull Papa in after her. I was the last to go. I did not hesitate for one more second. I threw myself through the wardrobe and fell headlong into the secret room.

Anneliese was there to shut the door behind me.

Chapter 13

I had bumped my arm hard as I flung myself through the wardrobe. When I stood up and looked down, an angry red bruise was already swelling on my elbow. It throbbed and ached, and I squeezed my eyes shut, counting silently in my head until the pain had eased up. Then, I opened my eyes and looked around.

All the workers were there, Anneliese and her sister, Herr Bromberger, Erna Haney, Willy Latter, along with all the others. Some people stood in the center of the floor, heads cradled in their hands. Others stood along the wall, pressing their backs into the concrete. I could see the looks on everyone's faces. Fear! It floated through the room like smoke from a fireplace when someone forgot to open the flue.

I guided Papa to a corner and stood next to him. I was worried about the bruise on his face that looked as sore as the one on my elbow. I clutched his arm, listening for sounds on the other side of the wardrobe. What was that? A muffled noise. Heavy boots. A man's voice, and then two more, or maybe three or four. Who knew how many soldiers were there, searching the factory! *Where is Herr Weidt?* I wondered wildly. *Is he trying to explain why his factory floor is empty on a work day? What possible excuse could he give? Will the soldiers take him away? What will happen to us next?*

I looked around the room again. Willy was rocking back and forth on his feet. Anneliese and Marianne stood holding one another. Herr Bromberger and Erna had their heads down. That was when Anneliese turned out the light, and the small room was plunged into blackness. Papa didn't flinch; darkness was something he was used to. For me, it was as if I myself were blind.

It was crowded in the small space with all of us jammed shoulder to shoulder. And it was cold. Frigid air seeped in through unseen cracks and soaked into my skin. The beautiful green dress that Anneliese had made for me was no protection. I longed for a sweater or a jacket to wrap myself in. But there had been no time to grab anything.

Despite the cold, a line of sweat trickled down my back, joined by another, and then a third. I tried to breathe in and out, but no air would enter my lungs. The harder I gasped for air, the less I was able to take in. I was shaking from head to toe, and I wanted my body to be anywhere other than in this room.

Papa placed his arm protectively around my shoulder and pulled my head closer, stroking my hair.

"Shhh," he whispered. "I'm here, always here."

That was when I reached up to touch the blue pin on my dress, my cornflower. *Mama*, I thought desperately. Not even Mama would be able to save us if we were found.

I had no idea how much time passed. Minutes? An hour? Eventually, the footsteps and voices faded on the other side of the cabinet. And still we stood and waited silently. And when more time had passed, I heard softer footsteps approaching and then the sound of jackets being pushed aside in the wardrobe. Finally, someone knocked on the secret door.

I held my breath.

The wardrobe door clicked open.

Chapter 14

Herr Weidt crawled into the secret room and stood up, light from the factory windows illuminating him from behind.

"The danger has passed, my friends," he said. "You can come back inside, now."

Still no one spoke. I squinted at the light, exhaled slowly, and reached up to wipe my brow. I had been sweating so hard that my hair was stuck to my forehead. Then I pulled Papa by the arm and we joined the line to crawl back through the wardrobe and reenter the factory. When we were back on the other side, Herr Weidt gathered us together into a circle.

"It was the Gestapo," he said grimly. "Three of them."

"But why?" I croaked out.

Herr Weidt sighed and scratched at his chin. "They're checking all the businesses. They know that there are Jews hiding all over the city."

My heart sank again. *It's only a matter of time*, I thought. *We may have avoided the Gestapo on this search, but how long can we keep doing it?*

"They were surprised to find an empty factory," Herr Weidt added.

"How did you get them to go away?" I asked.

"I told them that my workers had been working here late during the night, finishing off a big order. So, I had given everyone the morning off."

"And they believed you?"

"I've learned that these corrupt Gestapo officials will sometimes look the other way when you grease their palms," he said bitterly. "So, I slipped the head guard some money. I'll do anything to make sure they don't get close to you."

Would bribery really help? I wondered. And for how long?

"Back to your stations!" Herr Weidt instructed. "The best way to get over an incident like this is to go back to work."

One by one, the workers returned to their machines and tables. Slowly, the silent factory floor began to hum with activity once more. Bristles were combed and cut. Fibers were bound together and glued. Chairs scraped across the floor. Conversations resumed.

Herr Weidt walked among the workstations, pausing to talk to each worker. I watched as he placed a reassuring hand on Erna's shoulder. He said something to Herr Bromberger who reached out and eagerly shook his hand. Marianne and Anneliese both hugged him, which seemed to startle him so completely that his face turned bright red.

Papa went back to bundling horsehair. Herr Weidt paused to check the welt on his face.

"I heard that you tripped and fell. I hope you're all right," Herr Weidt said.

"It's nothing," Papa said, waving off the concern. "Lillian was there to help me. What would we do without you?" he added. "You're saving us over and over again."

Herr Weidt grasped both of Papa's hands and then moved over to me.

I stood in front of my packing boxes, but couldn't lift anything to put inside. My arms felt like stones, and my brain seemed disconnected from the rest of me. It was as if I were in pieces and couldn't put myself together.

Herr Weidt paused beside me. "Are you all right?" he asked.

"I don't know," I replied, hesitantly. "I think so. I mean, we weren't found, so yes, I'm fine."

He nodded forcefully. "And remember, the brushes and brooms we make here are necessary for the German military. As long as we continue to churn out these products, the Nazis will not shut me down, and everyone will have a safe place to work."

Safe! There was that word again.

"Anneliese told me that you hurt your arm," Herr Weidt said, suddenly.

I looked down at my elbow, which had swollen to nearly twice its usual size. And not only was my arm injured, but I realized that I had also torn the beautiful dress that Anneliese had given me. The sleeve hung from the seam at my shoulder. I winced as Herr Weidt gently took my arm and tried to straighten it.

"I don't think anything is broken," he said, as I explained about my fall trying to get through the wardrobe. "Ask Hetti to put some ice on it this evening. That should help bring the swelling down. You may have quite a colorful bruise there. You and your father," he added with a sad smile.

I pulled my arm back and cradled it against my body.

"Your father is lucky to have you with him," Herr Weidt added.

"We're lucky to have each other." I glanced over at Papa.

"But you're worried about him."

How does he know? "I don't want Papa to know that," I replied.

Herr Weidt sighed deeply and shook his head. "So many worries for a young girl."

He was just about to walk on, but I had a question that I still needed to ask. "Do you think they'll come back? The Gestapo, I mean." My voice was barely a whisper.

Herr Weidt nodded and sighed again. "I'm afraid so. But you're prepared now. You managed so well during this raid, and you'll manage just as well for the next one and the one after that."

How many more? I wondered.

Chapter 15

Hetti iced my elbow until I couldn't tell whether the blue color on my arm was from the bruise or from being frozen! And she fussed over Papa, trying to put ice on his cheek, though he really didn't want her to do that. Then, she fed us all evening long, insisting that the only solution to that terrible ordeal was to eat until we couldn't eat anymore.

"Food solves every problem, Mäuschen," she said, ladling another piece of roast chicken onto my plate and slathering it with thick gravy.

I didn't have the heart to say no to her. But I also couldn't swallow much of anything. In the end, I was grateful that she was there to care for us, to mother me in a way I needed.

But that night, as I was lying in bed, the memory of the search at the factory came crashing down on me. I reached for Schatzi, holding her close as I rocked back and forth trying to catch my breath. Tears streamed down my cheeks, but I didn't want to cry out for Papa. He had looked so sad and scared when we finally arrived back at Hetti's. I would have cried out for him in the past, but somehow, I couldn't do that anymore. So instead, I turned and reached for my cornflower pin, lying on the little table next to me, and pressed it against my cheek, longing for Mama. I was grateful that Hetti was trying to be motherly, but it wasn't the same. I needed my real mother. I wanted her with me, holding me, soothing me. Papa had said it was better that she wasn't alive to see all of this. But I wanted her alive!

Anneliese took back my torn dress and said she'd repair it. And, true to her promise, she returned it to me a few days later as good as new. I hugged her tightly but she brushed all my thanks aside.

"If only everything could be fixed as easily as this dress," she said.

Papa's cheek healed quickly. And, as Herr Weidt had predicted, my arm went from red to blue to bright purple. And then, as more weeks went by, the bruise turned to green, and then to lemon-yellow, and finally it faded to nothing. But the memory of the search did not fade one bit.

My life continued to exist in two places, Hetti's house where I ate and slept and grew accustomed to opera, and Herr Weidt's factory where I packaged boxes for shipment to the front and talked with my friends who were fast becoming my family. And of course, there was a third place, the walk to and from the factory where I kept my head down and held on to Papa. We always walked quickly, not wanting to be noticed.

Spring was trying desperately to appear after having been gone for the long winter. Some days it succeeded. The sun was warm, the wind was gentle, and tulip buds poked through the earth in the little boxes that hung from Hetti's windows. On other days the air was still icy cold, as if winter was hanging on with all its might, not wanting to disappear for the year.

There had been no more raids in the factory in those intervening weeks. But that did little to ease my fears. I lived with a never-ending, fierce belief that, any minute, the warning bell would ring, and we'd all have to make a mad dash for the secret room at the back of the factory. The fear was with me every day and all day long. I could never ignore it. It nagged at me, reminding me not to let my guard down.

I didn't say much to Papa about any of this. I could see that he was worried enough for himself, and of course, for me. His skin had become gray and sickly. And, despite Hetti's cooking, he looked as if he was losing weight. His jacket hung loosely on him, and I noticed that he had cinched in his belt to keep his trousers from falling down. I was afraid he might be getting sick. I knew he was sick with worry, and I didn't want to add to the burden that he was already feeling.

"How are you doing, my darling?" he would ask from time to time.

"I'm fine," I would lie. "I'm just so grateful that Herr Weidt is protecting us." That part, at least, was true.

In between all of this, there were moments that were unexpected and almost joyful. One day, Herr Weidt appeared in the factory carrying a big jug in his arms. He gathered all of us together.

"I've managed to find something that I think will be a treat for each one of you," he said.

Then, he reached for a small glass, tilted the jug, and

poured out a thick, golden looking liquid. He passed the glass from worker to worker. Each one took a small taste, smiled, and handed the glass along to the next person. When it was my turn, I held the glass in my hands and then sniffed cautiously at the liquid inside. There was something familiar about that smell; I couldn't quite tell what. Then I brought the glass up to my lips, tilted it back, and let the thick liquid pour across my tongue.

It was cool and sweet, and almost silky in my mouth. It wasn't honey; it was something else, I thought, desperately trying to place it. And then it came to me. Maple syrup! I couldn't remember the last time I had tasted this scrumptious liquid, not since all the trouble had started, not since Mama had died.

"Where did you get this?" I called out.

Herr Weidt smiled. "I can't give away all my secrets," he said. "I think it's best not to know everything."

He was right. It really didn't matter where it had come from. The important thing was that this was a moment when we could all laugh and be joyful and appreciate some sweetness.

Herr Weidt had some small jars and gave each of us a bit of syrup to take home.

Hetti made sweet pancakes that night that were

made even sweeter with the maple syrup that Herr Weidt had given us.

But that happy moment didn't last for long.

It was a cool day in April, 1942 when everything changed again.

Chapter 16

There was frost on the window that morning, a reminder of the last gasp of winter. Someone had left the windows of the factory open overnight, and it was as cold inside as it was outside, maybe colder. As soon as Papa and I arrived, I rushed around closing the windows up tight. But wintry air still hung in the building. I shivered, rubbing my hands together as I pulled my sweater closer around my body, and buttoned it up to my neck. Meanwhile, the other workers had all arrived. I was just about to start packaging a new order of brushes when the doors to the factory burst open with a loud bang. An icy wind flooded the room joined by four soldiers with rifles pointed in our direction. The Gestapo!

"Stop what you're doing!" one soldier shouted.

Workers who had their faces pressed down to the brushes they were assembling lifted their heads in the direction of the harsh command.

"We have orders to arrest all Jews. You're coming with us."

"No, no!" Papa cried. "You must know Otto Weidt? We work for him."

"We have permission to work here," I added. *Where was the warning bell? Where was the trusted friend who was meant to guard the door?*

"I don't care who your boss is. Someone tipped us off that there were Jews in this factory. And here you are. We've been ordered to round up all of you."

The soldier doing the talking was tall and thin as a pole. His black uniform hung loosely on his body as if it were three sizes too big.

"You can't hide from us anymore. *Los!* Out now!" the soldier bellowed.

My heart pounded in my chest like thunder, and my body shook from head to toe. This was my dreaded nightmare come true. Papa clutched my arm so tightly that I cried out in pain.

"I'm so sorry, my darling," he whispered, loosening his grip.

Just before leaving the factory, the soldier walked up to me. He stopped, inches from my face and stared into my eyes. He had a long, bony face that ended in a pointy chin. It was the first time that I noticed his cap with a pin in the shape of a skull and bones. It was the emblem of death. I flinched under his glare. Suddenly, he reached down and grabbed my blue cornflower pin, ripping it from the dress that Anneliese had made for me.

"What's this?" he asked, bringing the pin to his face and peering at it.

"No!" I cried. "Please, it was my mother's."

"Just a trinket," Papa added. "Won't you let my daughter keep it?"

The soldier stared at it another second. Thin lips curved into a devious smile. Then, he threw the pin down. It plunked onto the factory floor and rolled for a couple of seconds before stopping. "You won't need any jewelry where you're going."

I stared down at the floor where my pin lay. The yearning to reach down and grab it pulled at me with a force I could hardly resist. I glanced up at the guard and then back at the pin. All I needed was a second and then I would have it back. I pushed away my father's arm, and my own arm inched forward.

"No, Lillian! Don't!" Papa's sharp voice cut through my thoughts. He knew what I was thinking, as he always did. I stared again at my pin as every last bit of hope drained out of my body. Mama's pin, so dear to me, was lost—and so were we.

We grabbed coats and followed the soldiers out the door, through the streets of Berlin. Shopkeepers and café owners were just beginning to open their stalls and stores. They swept the pavement in front of their shops and turned their faces away from us. Men on their way to work quickly moved to the other side of the road, avoiding us altogether. Mothers shielded their children's eyes from staring.

"Hand on the shoulder of the person in front of you," Anneliese said, just as she had guided us to the back of the factory when the Gestapo had come to search. "I'm here if you need my help." This time her voice was shaky. She and her sister held on to each other. Herr Bromberger muttered that the end was near, which made me nearly sick to my stomach. Erna Haney was as pale as a ghostly moon. Only Willy Latter walked tall and said, "I won't let them see that I'm afraid."

We shuffled in a line, heads down, prodded by soldiers on all sides, and led by the skinny one in the ill-fitting uniform. If someone faltered or stepped out of the line, Anneliese was there to guide them back. I helped wherever I could, all the while never letting go of Papa's arm. We walked down Spandauer Strasse, crossing over the footbridge at the Spree River. With each step we moved farther and farther away from the factory and from Hetti's refuge. I wondered if Hetti knew what was happening to us. I hoped she didn't. It would break her heart. I thought about her, waiting for us that evening with a meal that would remain untouched. I thought about Mama who wasn't here to see all of this. And I thought about Ruth.

"My parents are getting more and more scared," Ruth *had said to me one day as we walked home from school many months ago. "They think we should try to get away."*

I nodded. "My Papa's worried too. But get away where?"

"I don't know. My parents aren't saying much to me. But I overheard them talk when I got up from bed to get some water last night. We have a cousin who lives in America."

"America!" My mouth dropped. "How would you even get there?"

"I don't know that either."

We walked in silence.

"If you go to America, how will I find you?" I finally asked.

Ruth looked at me, eyes full of hope. "Maybe you can come too?"

I gulped. Our home was here. Mama was buried here. Papa would never leave Berlin.

"Sure," I finally said.

We both knew that would never happen.

Ruth disappeared a week later.

On we walked, now on Leipziger Strasse, then turning this way and that for nearly an hour until we rounded a corner, and I could see the sign for the Anhalter Bahnhof, the train station from where people were deported to the concentration camps.

"Halt! Stop here!" the soldier finally ordered. Train cars waited in front of us in a long row.

Our line staggered to a stop. The soldiers gathered in a huddle to talk.

"What's happening?" Papa asked. Usually my father could hear the softest whisper a hundred paces away. But fear had blunted his senses.

"Shhh, Papa." I strained to listen, catching only a few words. I heard the soldiers say, "Theresienstadt," and then, "Get rid of them, once and for all."

We're doomed, I thought as my heart fell into my stomach. *The trains are headed for those terrible concentration camps. Soon, we'll be on board, and then our fate will be sealed.*

"What did they say?" Papa asked again.

"We're going to stay here for a while until they figure things out," I lied, keeping my voice as steady as I could. For once, I was grateful my father was blind. He couldn't see the tears pooling in my eyes. He couldn't see how my hands were shaking. And for once, he didn't seem to sense how I was feeling.

"I'm sure everything will be fine," Papa said. "We'll be back at the factory before you know it."

"Of course, we will." I squeezed my eyes shut, knowing we were both lying to each other.

Chapter 17

Time passed in an endless blur. One hour? Two? It was hard to tell. And still, we stood on the train station platform, huddled in a group, waiting for something to happen. The sky was filled with gray clouds that hung low in the air. *Any minute now, the rain will come*, I thought. *Our already-cold bodies will be drenched through.*

"Lean on me," Papa said, and I pressed closer to him.

I shivered again, feeling as though electricity was passing up and down my spine. My eyes searched the station platform, desperate for a way out. The guards had moved to unlock the train doors. Their backs were to us, their rifles lowered. I needed to do something, to take charge, to get us out of here. And then, an idea came to me, impossibly dangerous, but the only thing I could think of.

"We need to run away," I whispered to Papa.

"No!" he said, his voice rising.

"Shhh!" I glanced at the guards across the platform. This was the only moment we would have. With their backs to us, they might not notice if we slipped away and ran. *We could disappear into the morning crowd*, I thought, my mind racing wildly over this plan. *No one will pay attention to a young girl and her father.* I didn't know where we'd go after that, where we could hide.

Maybe we would find our way back to Hetti's house. She'd be so happy to see us. She'd pull us inside. She'd call me Mäuschen, and she'd make delicious food for me and Papa. And Schatzi would be waiting for me on my bed.

One step at a time, I thought shaking my head. *First, we need to get out of here. It's time to move.* "When I say go, I want you to start running," I commanded my father.

He pulled on my arm. "It won't work. I can't see where we're going, and you can't drag me fast enough."

"The soldiers aren't looking our way. They won't see us go." I took a step away from the platform.

Papa pulled me back again. "It's impossible!"

"But we have to try!" My resolve to run was turning to desperation. Of course, it was dangerous, maybe impossible, as Papa had said. But I wanted to make him agree that this was the only solution. "We're going to be taken away," I said. "The soldiers are getting the trains ready. You know what that means." I knew I didn't have to say more. Papa understood exactly what I was saying. Yet still, he resisted.

"They'll shoot us before we can take five steps," he said, his voice hopeless and filled with despair.

The guards were still inspecting the train. But, in another minute, they would come for us. *Being shot might be better than a different end*, I thought. *If we run, we might die. If we stay and get on the trains, we will die.* What choice did we have? No choice at all.

"And what about the others?" Papa said. "We can't leave them here."

I glanced at Anneliese and her sister, holding one another, foreheads touching, and at Erna, her head hanging so low I couldn't see her face. My heart sank once more. Papa was right. If we made a run for it, how could we leave our friends behind?

Herr Bromberger and Willy tried to sit, but just

as they were about to sink to the ground, the skinny soldier rushed over and ordered them to their feet.

"You're not here for a rest," he said, roughly.

The moment to get away had passed. There was no escape.

Chapter 18

The soldiers stood in front of the trains talking with each other as we continued to stand and wait. But this time there was a new voice among them, one that was familiar. I leaned forward, straining to hear once more, and caught the unmistakable voice of Herr Weidt! Where had he come from? At first, I couldn't hear what he was saying. He and the soldiers had their heads so close to each other. It was only when I saw him shake his fist in the air above his head that I realized how angry he was. And then, all the voices rose.

"What do you mean you've arrested the workers from my factory?" Herr Weidt demanded.

The skinny soldier who had led us here puffed out his chest. "We're under orders to arrest *all* Jews."

"I am Otto Weidt, a very important businessman in this city," Herr Weidt said, pulling himself up and glaring at the soldier. "I run the factory that makes brushes for the military...*your* army."

The soldier's eyes narrowed and scanned Herr Weidt from head to toe.

Herr Weidt ignored him. "I'm sure you've heard of me and my factory?"

"Well," the soldier replied. "I really don't—"

"The brushes I make are essential for the war effort," Herr Weidt interrupted. "I have orders from the *top* to produce these products." He punctuated that word, pointing a finger to the sky. "These blind men and women are the only ones who are trained to produce those brushes. And if my products don't get to the front, there will be trouble. Do you understand me?"

The soldier wrinkled his brow and shifted from one foot to the other. He glanced at the three others who were with him, each one avoiding Herr Weidt's stare.

Seconds turned to minutes while the soldier considered what had been said. Meanwhile, Herr Weidt stood absolutely still, staring at the soldier with a knife-like glare.

"Well?" Herr Weidt finally asked. "You're wasting precious time. I need these workers back at my factory."

The soldier shifted again, lowering his head, shaking it, then raising it once more. Meanwhile, Anneliese and her sister cried silent tears. Willy Latter still stood tall and straight. I held my breath. Suddenly, Erna moaned out loud, a low, deep, and desperate cry. And that snapped the soldier to attention.

"I don't care about your products. I've got my orders," he said, jutting his chin and matching Herr Weidt's stare.

Herr Weidt took a step forward. His face had tightened and his nostrils flared. "Your superiors won't be happy with you when they hear that you've arrested Otto Weidt's workers. Perhaps you didn't hear me before. I said, you'll be in big trouble with your superiors if my brushes stop getting to the army. Are you willing to take that risk?"

This time, the soldier frowned. He stepped back from Herr Weidt's glare, and ran a shaky hand across his forehead.

For a moment, I dared to think we might be saved. I thought that the soldier might set us free and let us return to the factory. I couldn't have been more wrong. A second later, he pulled himself together and faced Herr Weidt once more.

"Step aside. These Jews are getting on this train, and I don't care what happens to them after that."

My stomach clenched as the soldiers surrounded us.

"Move forward. Don't stop!" they ordered.

The train doors slid open on their rollers with a loud bang. We shuffled toward the blackness inside. My throat was so tight I could barely breath. A voice in my head was screaming, *Don't let us die.*

The skinny soldier pushed Papa from behind. He stumbled and nearly fell.

"Papa!" I screamed.

"Stay next to me, Lillian."

"I'm here. I won't leave you." I clutched my father.

The open door to the train was only steps away, ten more, then five, then two. In another moment, we would be inside the blackness. My legs twitched with fear as I moved forward.

Anneliese whimpered.

"I thought I was safe," Erna muttered.

The life in Herr Bromberger's eyes had faded.

The open train door was right in front of us. The thumping of my heart rose up into my throat. Another shove from behind, and Willy Latter was the first to step up. Herr Bromberger followed, head still low. Erna wailed and then lifted herself up to join them. Papa and I were the next in line.

And that's when Herr Weidt called out to the skinny soldier once more.

"Wait, my friend," he said. "Let's start again."

I'm not sure what made the soldier stop. But this time, instead of pushing Papa and me into the train, he turned. Something had changed, something that—at first—I didn't understand. Suddenly, Herr Weidt was smiling as he stepped forward and threw an arm around the startled soldier's shoulder. He pulled the soldier away from the rest of us and huddled with him. I could still make out what they were saying.

"I have something here that might interest you." Herr Weidt reached into his jacket pocket and pulled out a small glass bottle. "Do you have a wife?" he asked.

The soldier nodded, still wary.

"This is the finest perfume in all of Berlin. And there's more where this came from. Just release my Jewish workers, and I'll bring you more bottles."

Herr Weidt was trying to bribe the guard into letting us go, just like he had during the raid of the factory weeks earlier. But would it work this time? These Gestapo soldiers were so far past the point of looking the other way.

The soldier reached out to touch the bottle of perfume. "What do you care what happens to these Jews?" he asked. "You can get some more. Besides, they're blind. They're worth even less than others."

In spite of my fear, I felt a flash of anger. He was talking about my father and the others like they were scraps of garbage.

The soldier still hesitated as Herr Weidt held out the perfume. "You'll be a hero at home with this. And if that's not enough, I'll make sure that a crate of champagne is delivered to you first thing in the morning."

The soldier glanced over at us; three already on the train, and the others standing at the open doors. Then he looked over at Herr Weidt and down at the perfume bottle, back and forth, up and down. We waited. A minute passed and then another.

"What's happening?" Papa asked one more time.

"Don't say a word, Papa," I whispered. "Herr Weidt is trying to figure this out."

"Champagne, you say?" The soldier's voice was curious.

"Only the finest in all of Berlin. You'd enjoy that, wouldn't you?"

The soldier shifted his gaze back at his comrades,

then over at us, then at Herr Weidt. The other soldiers raised their heads, curious as to what was happening.

"What are you staring at?" the skinny soldier called out to them. "Guard the prisoners!"

The soldiers turned to us once more. I stretched my neck, desperate to hear what Herr Weidt would do next. But now, it was harder to hear his conversation with the skinny soldier. Their heads were bent toward one another. I could only catch a few words. "Between you and me," I heard Herr Weidt say. And then, "No one else will know."

And still we waited, Erna Haney, Herr Bromberger, and Willy Latter on the train. Papa, me, Anneliese, her sister, and the others still on the platform. The cold and wind wrapped itself around us.

And then, I watched as the skinny soldier pulled a small piece of paper from his pocket and wrote something on it. He handed the paper to Herr Weidt, who folded his fingers around it, and said, "I'll make the delivery to this address tomorrow."

Finally, the soldier pulled his shoulders back and grabbed the bottle of perfume. "*Jawohl*, okay," he said, raising his voice. "Get them out of here before I change my mind!"

Just before turning away from the soldier, Herr Weidt said, "By the way." And then he tapped his temple, just like he had done when he first spoke to me in the factory so many months earlier, and he said to the soldier, "Just so you know, I am quite blind, too. And I think my life has great value, just like the lives of the people over there."

The guard's jaw dropped open as Herr Weidt rushed over to us. "Get off the train," he hissed to the three who stood above us. Willy Latter and Herr Bromberger jumped down and turned to help Erna back onto the platform.

"Hold on to each other," Herr Weidt said in a low and urgent voice. "Perhaps I shouldn't have provoked that guard, but I couldn't help myself. I had to tell him off, for all of us! Now, we need to leave before he changes his mind."

"My Papa said you'd come for us," I whispered. "And here you are."

Herr Weidt smiled briefly and reached out to place something in my hand. When I looked down, there was my cornflower pin.

I gasped and looked up at Herr Weidt. "But how...?"

"I felt something under my foot when I arrived at

the factory and discovered that you had all been taken away. I heard it rattle on the floor and when I reached down to see what it was, I found your pin. I thought you might want it back."

Tears blurred my vision. I reached up with shaky hands to attach the pin to my dress, right where it belonged.

Finally, Herr Weidt faced our whole group. "I need to get you out of here. Now!"

I didn't hesitate for another second. I grabbed Papa with one arm and he reached out to Anneliese with the other. She clutched her sister, who took Herr Bromberger's hand. He grabbed Willy Latter, who linked arms with Erna Haney, and so on, until we were joined together as one human chain. And then, with Herr Weidt in the lead, we marched away from the train station and back to the safety of the factory.

What Really Happened

If you walk down a narrow lane off Rosenthaler Strasse in the Mitte district of Berlin, you will find yourself in a small, rather unassuming courtyard, cobblestones on the ground, a few low-rise buildings, one café, and a couple of trees. In the middle and to one side is a plain gray door. It looks as if it might be the entrance to an apartment. But the sign in front tells a different story. It reads *Museum Blindenwerkstatt Otto Weidt*, Museum Otto Weidt's Workshop for the Blind.

In 2018, I visited this small museum, inspired to write a book about the man who, I discovered, had protected dozens of blind Jewish men and women by employing them in his factory and saving many of them from deportation to the concentration camps.

Otto Weidt

In 1936, Otto Weidt opened this factory and began to manufacture brooms and brushes. He had learned the trade of brushmaking when he himself lost much of his sight as a teenager. When the Second World War began in 1939, Otto had his factory classified by the Nazi government as "essential for the war effort." Many of his products were made to order for the armed forces of Nazi Germany, led by Adolf Hitler. Despite the fact that Otto was providing supplies to the German army, he was strongly opposed to the beliefs of the Nazi party. In particular, he could see how badly Jewish people were being treated, and he vowed to do as much as he could to help these persecuted people. He began to employ both deaf and blind Jewish workers in his factory. He provided food and organized hiding places to protect them from deportation to the concentration camps. He sent supplies to Jews who had already been imprisoned in these places. He bribed the police and Nazi officials to release Jews who had been arrested.

His commitment to protecting these blind and deaf Jews was all the more remarkable for the fact that the Nazi government was determined to do away with anyone, Jewish or Christian, with a disability. These individuals were not "worthy" to be part of the

"Master Race" that the Nazis wanted to create. Those with disabilities were often labeled as "life unworthy of life."

The Otto Weidt Factory is small, not at all what one might imagine a factory to look like. Three or four long narrow rooms follow each other and end in a small room that was used to hide the Jewish workers when the Gestapo would search the factory looking for Jews. A large wardrobe had once been placed in front of this back room to disguise it as a hiding place.

Throughout the museum are brief stories about the many Jewish people whom Otto Weidt protected. I spent hours reading the small and often incomplete biographies, thinking about how I could weave the lives of some of these real people into the story I wanted to write.

In real life, there were the Jewish twins, Anneliese and Marianne Bernstein. They had come to Berlin in 1940, wanting to learn a trade. Anneliese became a dressmaker, and Marianne, who was blind, trained as a brushmaker in Otto's factory. They remained safe until 1943. When it became too dangerous for them to continue working at the factory, they went into hiding, often sleeping in parks to avoid being on the streets. They eventually left Berlin and found refuge with farmers in the Breslau area. They survived the war and immigrated to the United States in 1946.

I learned about Willy Latter who became blind at the age of thirteen when surgeons bungled his "routine" eye surgery. He was a concert pianist and music teacher whose wife and two daughters were in hiding when he came to work in Otto's factory. Willy's wife was not Jewish, but had converted to Judaism when they married. Willy, his wife, and their children survived the Nazi persecution and left for the United States after the war. Willy passed away in 1974 at the age of seventy-eight.

There was Erna Haney, who had been born blind in 1895 in Lissa, Poland. She moved to Berlin in 1911 and worked for many years as a secretary. She married in 1921 and had two sons. At first, she and her family were spared from Nazi persecution because her husband was Catholic. But eventually, her husband and sons went into hiding, and Erna went to work in Otto's factory. She and her family survived the war. Erna passed away in 1990 at the age of ninety-four.

Another wonderful true story was about a woman named Hedwig Porschütz, known to many as Hetti. Born in 1890, Hetti started out working in Otto's stockroom. For years, she housed and fed Jewish

Otto Weidt and his workshop employees, 1942

workers from the factory, including for a time the twins Anneliese and Marianne Bernstein. She was eventually arrested and sentenced to eighteen months in prison. However, the conviction was not for hiding Jews. She was convicted of hoarding food! She never revealed the Jews she had protected. She served her sentence at the Zillerthal-Erdmannsdorf labor camp in Germany from October 1944 until the end of the war.

Many of the dozens of Jewish workers who were protected in Otto's factory survived the war. Some were not as lucky. Among those who perished in the death camps was Bernhard Bromberger. He was born in 1877 in Adelnau, Poland. He married and had three sons and a daughter. He served as a soldier in the First World War, then moved to Berlin where he opened a textile shop. He became blind from an eye ailment as a young man. His four children managed to escape from Berlin as the war was ramping up. They found refuge in Shanghai, China, one of the only places in the world to accept Jewish refugees who were trying to escape persecution in Europe. Herr Bromberger and his wife chose not to leave their home, and he began working in Otto's factory. In 1943, Herr Bromberger and his wife were deported to the death camp, Auschwitz, where they were killed.

There were many more stories like these that I read while I visited the Otto Weidt museum in 2018. It was difficult to choose which ones I wanted to include in the book. I knew I had to create a fictional father and his daughter, a girl whom I named Lillian Frey, who came to Otto for help. The truth is there were no children who worked in Otto's factory.

It is unclear exactly how many Jewish people Otto protected. There are more than thirty stories documented in the museum, but possibly many more passed through the factory whose names and stories were lost. The real people whom I wrote about represent the dozens that Otto helped. Some survived, but some could not avoid eventual arrest and deportation.

After the war, Otto helped establish a Jewish home for children who had been orphaned during the Holocaust. He died of heart failure in 1947 at the age of sixty-four. He was one of those remarkable individuals who was willing to risk his own life to help Jews in need. In 1971, he was recognized as Righteous Among the Nations, the highest honor that Israel bestows upon those who saved Jews during the Holocaust.

Acknowledgments

Huge thanks, as always, to Margie Wolfe of Second Story Press, publisher extraordinaire! Margie's advice, encouragement, and support of my writing is unwavering. I don't take that for granted, and am eternally grateful for it all. Special thanks to the wonderful women of SSP: Emma Rodgers, Melissa Kaita, Phuong Truong, and Kathryn Cole.

It was a pleasure to work with Sarah Swartz who edited this book ever so carefully and meticulously. Her knowledge of Germany only added to the authenticity of the story.

And to my family—Ian, Gabi, Jake, and my newest "children," Vanessa and Jeremy—I love and cherish you all.

About the Author

KATHY KACER is the author of numerous books that tell true stories of the Holocaust for young readers of all ages, including *The Secret of Gabi's Dresser*, *The Brave Princess and Me*, and *To Look a Nazi in the Eye*. Her books have won many awards, including the Silver Birch, the Red Maple, the Hackmatack, and the Jewish Book Award. A former psychologist, Kathy has traveled the globe speaking to children and adults about the importance of keeping the memory of the Holocaust alive. She lives in Toronto.